This
book is
dedicated to all the children in the
world, to all the muffins,
homeless people,
birds, seeds, rain and flowers
in the world.

Giora Carmi

A CIRCLE OF FRIENDS

BY Giora Carmi

Star Bright Books
New York

Printed in China   9   8   7   6   5   4   3   2   1

Hardback ISBN-13: 978-1-932065-00-8   ISBN-10: 1-932065-00-8
Paperback ISBN-13: 978-1-59572-060-3   ISBN-10: 1-59572-060-X

Designed by Jin Choi

Library of Congress Cataloging-in-Publication Data

Carmi, Giora.
    A circle of friends / by Giora Carmi.
        p. cm.
    Summary: When a boy anonymously shares his snack with a homeless man, he begins a
cycle of good will.
    ISBN 1-932065-00-8
    [1. Sharing--Fiction. 2. Stories without words.] I. Title.

PZ7.K1425Ci 2003
[E]--dc21
                                                              2002042879